Maya Prays for Rain

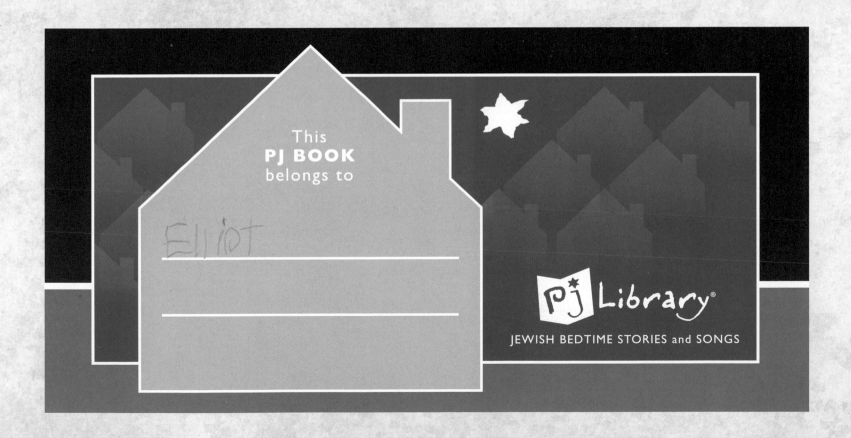

D0132340

For Annie, Livy, Gideon, and Nathan—ST

To my loves Santiago, Patricio, Ana and Maria—AO

KAR-BEN PUBLISHING, INC.
A division of Lerner Publishing Group, Inc.
241 First Avenue North
Minneapolis, MN 55401 USA
1-800-4-KARBEN

Website address: www.karben.com

Main body text set in ChurchwardSamoa Light 16/20.
Typeface provided by Chank.

Library of Congress Cataloging-in-Publication Data

Names: Tarcov, Susan, author. | Ochoa, Ana, illustrator.
Title: Maya prays for rain / by Susan Tarcov ; illustrated by Ana Ochoa.
Description: Minneapolis, MN : Kar-Ben Publishing, a division of Lerner Publishing Group, [2016] | 2016
Identifiers: LCCN 2015040983 (print) | LCCN 2015041776 (ebook) | ISBN 9781467789295 (lb : alk. paper) | ISBN 9781467794114 (pb : alk. paper) | ISBN 9781512409444 (eb pdf)
Subjects: LCSH: Shemini Atzeret—Juvenile literature. | Sukkot—Juvenile literature.
Classification: LCC BM695.S53 T37 2016 (print) | LCC BM695.S53 (ebook) | DDC 296.7/2—dc23
LC record available at http://lccn.loc.gov/2015040983

Manufactured in Hong Kong
1 – PN – 4/29/16

091628.2K1/B0899/A5

Maya Prays for Rain

Susan Tarcov

illustrations by Ana Ochoa

KAR-BEN
PUBLISHING

It was an unusually bright and sunny day, even though it was fall. Maya was on her way to drop off some homework for her friend Wendy, who was sick with a cold.

"What a beautiful day," thought Maya as she walked along. "Too bad Wendy isn't feeling well." The leaves were beginning to turn and the sky was a bright blue.

Mrs. Cisneros was in her yard hanging clothes on the clothesline. "Nothing smells as good as clothes that have dried in the sunshine, Maya," she said. "And it's good for the earth."

The Papadakis family was loading baskets and coolers into the trunk of their car. "We're going on a picnic, Maya!" they said. "The weather is so beautiful. We'll be back tonight."

Mr. Patel was painting his fence. "I'm using slow-drying paint, Maya," he said. "Slow-drying paint lasts longer. On a day like today it will have plenty of time to dry."

Mrs. Kelly was in her yard putting up party decorations. "It's Megan's birthday, Maya," she said. "Since it's such a nice day, we're having the party outdoors!"

Tommy Bilecki was filling a tub with water. "I'm giving Biscuit a bath, Maya," he said. "Biscuit hates the hair dryer. Today he can shake himself dry."

Nadia Ali was on her porch with a big container. "I'm releasing my butterflies today, Maya," she said. "I was waiting for a day with perfect weather. They can't fly if their wings get wet."

Jason Hu was running to join his baseball team in the park. "It's the semifinals, Maya!" he called. "Wish us luck."

"Good luck, Jason!"
Maya waved as she crossed
the street to Wendy's house.

"Hi, Maya," snuffled Wendy as she opened the door. "Is your family going to the synagogue today for Shemini Atzeret services? I can't go, but I like this holiday. It's the one where we pray for rain!"

"For rain!" Maya cried. "Oh no! Feel better, Wendy—I have to go tell the neighbors!" And she rushed off to warn everyone.

"Jason, postpone your game!" she called. "It's going to rain!"

"The game's already started, Maya," Jason said. "We have to play five innings or it doesn't count."

"Nadia, don't release your butterflies! It's going to rain!"

But the butterflies were already flitting among the flowers.

"Tommy, don't give Biscuit a bath.
It's going to rain!"

But Biscuit was already up
to his ears in suds.

"Mrs. Kelly, take down the party decorations. It's going to rain!"

"Oh, dear," Mrs. Kelly said. "It would take me forever to gather up all the treasures I hid for the treasure hunt. I'll just have to hope for the best!"

"Mr. Patel, switch to quick-drying paint. It's going to rain!"

"I can't switch in the middle," Mr. Patel said. "It wouldn't look right."

At the Papadakis house, Maya hollered, "Don't go
on your picnic—it's going to rain!"

But the Papadakis family car was already gone.

"Mrs. Cisneros, take down your clothes. It's going to rain!" But all the clothes were already hanging on the line. Maya knocked on Mrs. Cisneros's front door. Then she knocked on Mrs. Cisneros's back door. But Mrs. Cisneros wasn't home.

Maya ran to the synagogue. "Rabbi, let's not pray for rain," she begged. "Mrs. Cisneros has clothes on her clothesline, the Papadakis family has gone on a picnic, Mr. Patel is painting his fence with slow-drying paint, Mrs. Kelly is planning an outdoor party for Megan's birthday, Tommy Bilecki is giving his dog a bath, Nadia Ali just released her butterflies—oh, and Jason Hu's baseball team has to play five innings or it doesn't count!"

The rabbi smiled. "You can relax, Maya. When we pray for rain today, we're not praying for the rain to fall *here*. We're praying for it to fall *in Israel!* This is the start of the rainy season in Israel, and we want Israel to have lots of rain so crops and trees will grow. Jews always pray for it to rain in Israel on Shemini Atzeret—no matter where we live—to show our love for Israel."

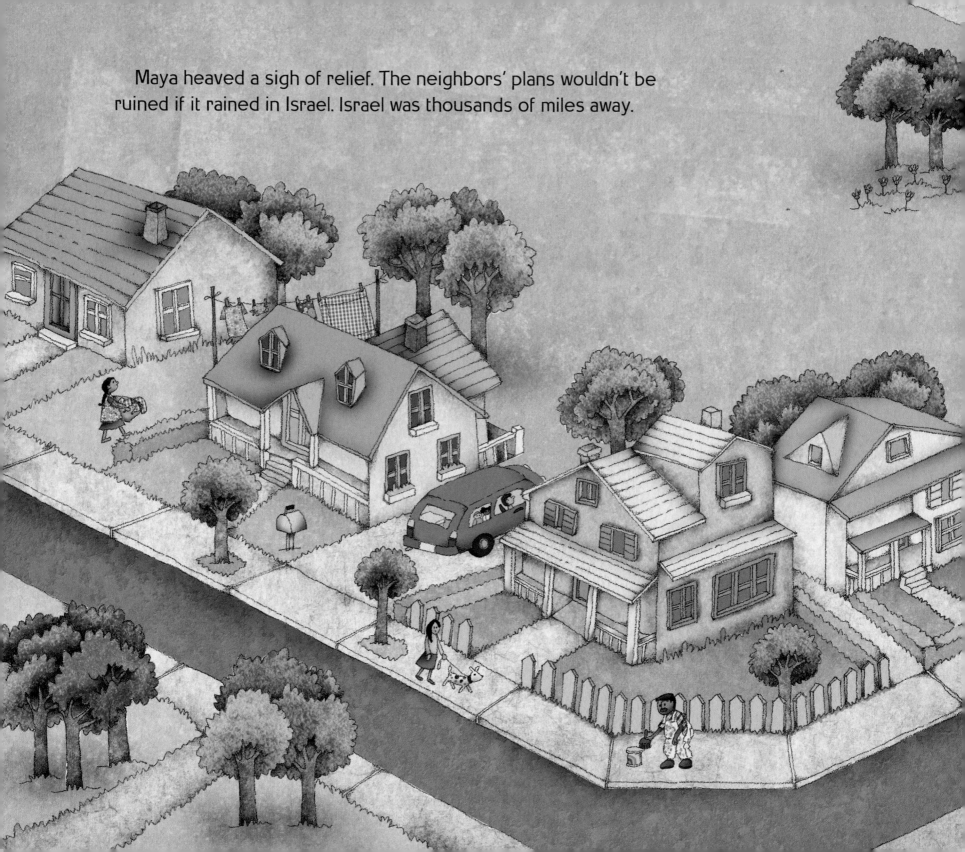

Maya heaved a sigh of relief. The neighbors' plans wouldn't be ruined if it rained in Israel. Israel was thousands of miles away.

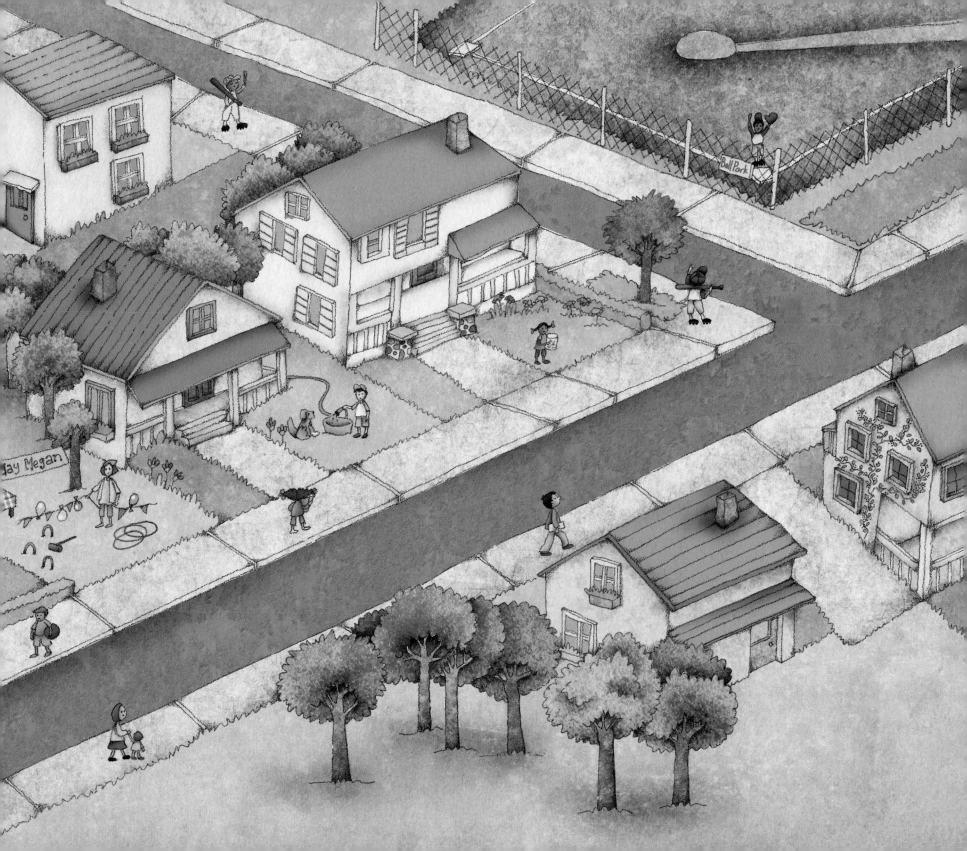

During services, Maya sat with her family in the synagogue while the rabbi led the prayer for rain: "You are our God, who causes the wind to blow and the rain to fall."

And Maya happily said, "Amen."

About Shemini Atzeret

The holidays of Shemini Atzeret and Simchat Torah fall at the end of Sukkot. In Israel they are celebrated on a single day; outside of Israel they are celebrated as two separate holidays. While these holidays are often thought of as part of Sukkot, they are actually separate holidays. Shemini Atzeret means "the assembly of the eighth day" as it falls after the seven days of Sukkot. Part of the Shemini Atzeret service is a prayer for rain, since the holiday comes at the beginning of Israel's rainy season. This prayer is our request for the seas of Israel to fill and the crops to grow, providing food and water for the people of Israel. (We recite this prayer after Sukkot is over because we'd like nice weather during Sukkot so we can enjoy the time in our sukkah.) Before sundown on Shemini Atzeret, it is customary to go into the sukkah, have a snack, and say good-bye to the sukkah until next year.

Susan Tarcov grew up next to the Bronx Zoo, a great inspiration for writing children's books. She is married, has three children and lives in Chicago.

Ana Ochoa was born and raised in Mexico City. She studied Graphic Design in Mexico and illustration in France. Her work has been exhibited in Tokyo, Bologna, Taiwan, New Delhi, Colombia, Bratislava, Rio de Janeiro and Mexico City. She loves traveling and living in other countries, reading French comic books and visiting flea markets. She lives in Mexico City.